THE SPY FIVE

OPERATION PHANTOM DRIBBLER

by **Spencer Strange**

with

Andrea Menotti — *words*

and

pictures — **Kelly Kennedy**

Scholastic Inc.

New York Toronto London Auckland Sydney
Mexico City New Delhi Hong Kong Buenos Aires

Visit the Spy Five web site at
www.scholastic.com/spyfive
Your new password is:
coolcatch

Stop by and send the Spy Five an e-mail. We love to hear from you!

Use this password to access a new game!

ISBN 0-439-70357-3

Copyright © 2005 by Scholastic Inc.

Design: Julie Mullarkey Gnoy

12 11 10 9 8 7 6 5 4 3 2   5 6 7 8 9/0

Printed in the U.S.A.

First printing, May 2005

2

CHAPTERS

CHAPTER 1
JULIAN'S TEAM DREAM

"**Y**ou know what our school needs more than *anything*?" Julian asked one day when we were walking home.

"What?" I asked.

"A basketball team," Julian said.

"That'd be great," I agreed. "But I bet Mr. Naulty wouldn't think so."

Julian rolled his eyes at the mention of our obnoxious principal. Mr. Naulty was pretty much always against anything fun.

"My *cousin's* school has a basketball team," Julian said. "*And* a track team. They get *all* the good stuff."

"Maybe we could do something like we did before, with the field trip to the museum," I said. "You know, get one of the teachers to back us up."

"Like who?" Julian asked.

"Well," I said, hesitating because I knew Julian wouldn't like my idea, "the obvious choice would be Mr. Davidson—"

"Oh *please*," Julian said. "Are you insane?"

Mr. Davidson is our gym teacher, and Julian doesn't exactly like him (the understatement of the century).

"It might be worth a try," I said.

"No way," Julian said, shaking his head firmly. "He doesn't care about basketball. He just cares about *girl stuff*."

Mr. Davidson

Julian was *always* saying stuff like that about Mr. Davidson. You see, Mr. Davidson and Julian have very different opinions about what should happen in gym class:

JULIAN'S OPINION

MR. DAVIDSON'S OPINION

ALL BASKETBALL, ALL THE TIME

STRETCHES

SIT-UPS

AEROBICS

MIME STUFF

SQUARE DANCING

We had one unit on basketball for a couple of weeks at the beginning of the year, and Julian was real happy. But then things took a turn for the worse (as far as Julian was concerned) when Mr. Davidson decided to teach us all how to be mimes.

Yes, *mimes*—those people who act stuff out without saying anything, kind of like clowns but without the curly wigs and red noses.

Mr. Davidson is a professional mime, you see. I'm not exactly sure how he ended up being a gym teacher, but we were stuck with him. So, we learned a bunch of mime things, like how to pretend we were touching a wall:

And we learned how to make it look like we were going down an escalator:

Personally, I thought it was kind of interesting. Or at least funny. But Julian wasn't having *any* of it. He was especially upset because we only had gym class one day a week for forty-five minutes, so the time was really precious. It was the only time all week we got to be in the gym (it was locked anytime classes weren't in there). Considering that the gym had a full basketball court and four extra side hoops, it was like torture for Julian to be in there and not play basketball.

Things were pretty tense all year long, but *nothing* compared to the day when Mr. Davidson started teaching us aerobics. *That* was a totally unforgettable day, because right when Mr. Davidson started showing us the "pony trot," Julian had a major explosion.

"I'M NOT DOING THE PONY TROT!" he yelled.

And then Julian said something else. Something even *worse*. Something that made the whole class get dead quiet, which was rare, because no one was *ever* quiet in Mr. Davidson's class.

And, of course, Mr. Davidson got real upset. He made Julian come in for a "private chat" after class, *and* he called Julian's grandma and told her everything.

The end result was that Julian got in huge trouble with his grandma and wasn't allowed to play basketball or video games for two weeks. After that, Julian decided that Mr. Davidson was the Worst Teacher Ever to Exist on this Planet.

It was too bad, because out of all of our teachers, Mr. Davidson was probably the best bet to help us start a school basketball team. It was just a matter of convincing Julian....

* * * *

The next day after lunch, I told the rest of the Spy Five about Julian's basketball team idea. They were all for it.

"Definitely," Anika said. "I know a *lot* of people who'd want to be on the team."

"That's what I'm saying," Julian said. "*Everyone* wants a basketball team."

"Are you talking about just a *guys'* team or a girls' team, too?" Ursula asked.

"I think we should have *both*," Anika answered for Julian. "And a dance team to perform at halftime."

"*And* a person in charge of selling refreshments for profit," Ursula suggested.

Ursula's refreshment stand

"And a person in charge of *using* the profits to outfit the gym with a state-of-the-art scoreboard and audio system," Blitz added.

Blitz's scoreboard and audio system

SCORE!

"We'll *discuss* the use of the profits," Ursula said, looking at Blitz with narrowed eyes.

"Anyway, guys," I said, "we figured the first step would be to convince one of the teachers to help us out."

"MR. DAVIDSON!" everyone yelled (except Julian).

Julian just glowered.

"You think *he's* gonna help with a *basketball team?*" Julian demanded. "*Mr. Mime?*"

"*I* think he'd help," Ursula said. "We did a unit on basketball back in the fall, remember?"

"Yeah, for like, five *minutes*," Julian said. "He hates basketball."

"He *likes* basketball," Anika argued. "He just teaches other stuff, too."

"LIKE HOW TO PRETEND YOU'RE RIDING AN ESCALATOR?" Julian blasted.

"I actually found that interesting," Ursula said.

"Gimme a break," Julian shot back.

"Can't you at least give him a chance?" Anika asked Julian. "It's not like he's mean and nasty or anything."

"*I* think he'd help," Blitz chimed in.

"And considering the gym is like his *classroom*, he's definitely the one we should talk to first, since the team would have to use the gym," Ursula insisted.

"And if *that* doesn't work, we can talk to someone else," I said.

Julian still wasn't happy, but after a little more convincing, he agreed to give it a try.

CAN'T YOU AT LEAST GIVE HIM A CHANCE? IT'S NOT LIKE HE'S MEAN AND NASTY OR ANYTHING.

CHAPTER 2
A CHAT WITH MR. MIME

We all went to talk to Mr. Mime—I mean Mr. Davidson—in his office that day after school. To our complete and utter shock, he said, right away:

"I think that's an excellent idea. I'm all for it."

"**REALLY?**" we all said.

"Absolutely," Mr. Davidson said. "I've always felt we should have sports teams. In fact, I've already started discussing the issue with Mr. Naulty."

"**YOU HAVE?**"

"Yup," Mr. Davidson said. "I mentioned it to him a few months ago, right after I spoke with Julian about his...um...*strong feelings* about basketball. Mr. Naulty said he'd consider starting a team if there was enough interest."

"**HE DID?**"

We were all in shock. Mr. Naulty would actually consider allowing something *fun*?

"There's *definitely* enough interest!" Julian practically shouted, like he couldn't believe Mr. Davidson would ever think anything else.

"Well, good," Mr. Davidson said with a smile. "Then we should be able to make a good case to Mr. Naulty. And you know what *else* would help?"

"What?" we asked.

"Mr. Naulty's always worried about the budget, so it would be good if we could come up with ways to do our own fundraising to afford uniforms and things like that," Mr. Davidson said.

"I can do that!" Ursula burst out. "That's one of my specialties!"

"Great," Mr. Davidson said. "Sounds like we'll be able to make this happen, then!"

Wow, that was easy. And if it was *so* easy, I had to ask...

"How come the school never had a team before?"

"Well, actually, the school *did* have a basketball program several years ago," Mr. Davidson said, reaching to his back shelf and picking up a dusty cardboard photo holder. He opened it up and showed us a picture of a boys' basketball team.

"This picture was taken the last year of the basketball program," Mr. Davidson continued, "six years ago."

"Why did it end?" I asked.

"Well, unfortunately, there was...a tragedy," Mr. Davidson said.

"What happened?" we all asked.

"Sadly, the coach died," Mr. Davidson said with a wince.

"He DIED?" we all asked. "HOW?"

Have you ever noticed that people always have to know *how* somebody died?

"He had a heart attack, I think," Mr. Davidson said. "It was a real shame. He was a very nice man, apparently. His name was Mr. Camacho. The kids loved him. Mr. Naulty really liked him, too. I think they were actually good friends."

"Wow," we all said.

Mr. Camacho must have been a *really* great guy, to be popular with both kids *and* Mr. Naulty. That's totally unheard of.

"The gym teacher who was hired to replace Mr. Camacho wasn't interested in continuing the basketball program," Mr. Davidson said, "so that was the end of that, since none of the other teachers wanted to do it."

"That must've been really sad," Anika said.

"I'm sure it was," Mr. Davidson said. "That was all before my time."

"When did you get here?" I asked.

"Two years ago," Mr. Davidson said. "Actually, when I moved into this office, a lot of Mr. Camacho's old things were still here, like that photo, some books, and those trophies on the shelf over there."

We all went over to look at the trophies. Pretty impressive.

"And this is actually his clipboard," Mr. Davidson added, holding up his own clipboard, which had "CAMACHO" printed along the bottom.

"You're using his *clipboard*?" Blitz asked, looking kind of queasy.

"Why not?" Mr. Davidson asked. "It's a perfectly good clipboard."

We all stared at the thing like it was haunted. I think it was the same one Mr. Camacho was holding in the team photo.

"This is his stopwatch, too," Mr. Davidson added, holding up his stopwatch. "Found it in the desk drawer. Works great."

We all winced.

"Oh, come on," Mr. Davidson said. "I'm sure Mr. Camacho would want his things to go to good use. What's wrong with that?"

We all shrugged.

"It's just kind of weird," Anika said. "Kind of haunting or something."

"*Haunting?*" Mr. Davidson repeated. "You know, for some reason, I hear a lot about haunting when it comes to Mr. Camacho these days."

"What do you mean?" I asked.

"Oh, nothing," Mr. Davidson said, shaking his head and rolling his eyes.

"Come on," we all pressed.

"Well, if you *really* want to know," Mr. Davidson finally said, "I heard a rumor recently that the gym is haunted by some *Phantom Dribbler*."

"A PHANTOM DRIBBLER?" we all blasted.

"Oh, I'm sure it's nothing," Mr. Davidson said with a laugh. "Do you know Kelvin, the janitor?"

"Yeah," we all said.

We knew Kelvin from some operations we'd done earlier in the year, like our cafeteria investigation. He was always really nice to us.

"Well, Kelvin says he's heard dribbling coming from the gym in the afternoon, but when he opens the door, no one's in there," Mr. Davidson said.

"REALLY?" we all asked.

"That's what he says," Mr. Davidson said, shaking his head. "But it was probably *me* he heard, you know. I shoot hoops in the gym after school sometimes."

Kelvin

"For *real?*" Julian asked, looking surprised.

"Sure," Mr. Davidson said. "I sometimes play after I've locked up the gym for the day. And when the gym door's locked, it takes a while for Kelvin to get it open, because he has to get the keys from the main office. In the amount of time it would take him to get the keys, I could have left the gym through the street exit."

We all nodded. That seemed fair enough.

"What does Kelvin think of that?" I asked.

"Oh, he's not convinced," Mr. Davidson said, shaking his head.

"He thinks it's...Mr. Camacho's *ghost?*" Blitz asked with raised eyebrows.

"He suggested that," Mr. Davidson said with a shrug. "But I hope he wasn't serious. You don't believe in that kind of stuff, do you?"

"No," Julian, Ursula, Anika, and I said quickly.

But Blitz looked like he wasn't so sure.

"It's nothing for you to be concerned about anyway," Mr. Davidson said firmly. "We need to focus on getting our basketball program together, right?"

"Right," we said, nodding quickly.

And so we said our good-byes and thank-yous and left Mr. Davidson's office.

But, of course, we were not *about* to let the matter of the Phantom Dribbler go uninvestigated. No way.

And so our next operation began.

CHAPTER 3
NO OTHER WAY OUT

Right after we talked to Mr. Davidson, we went to find Kelvin. We checked all the floors and finally found him downstairs in the cafeteria.

IT'S THE PRIVATE-EYE SPIES!

"It's the private-eye spies!" Kelvin announced as we approached. He had all kinds of names for us like that.

"We've been looking for you *everywhere*," Anika said.

"Why?" Kelvin asked.

"'Cause we wanna hear about the Phantom Dribbler!" Blitz blurted out.

Kelvin's eyes got really wide.

"How'd you hear about *that?*" Kelvin asked.

"Mr. Davidson told us," I said.

"He *did?*" Kelvin asked. "I'm surprised he mentioned it. He told *me* he was sure I'd just heard *him* playing ball."

"He still thinks that," Ursula said. "But we want to hear *your* side of it."

"Yeah," everyone else nodded.

"Can you tell us the whole story?" Anika asked.

"All right," Kelvin shrugged.

"We want all the details," Ursula said, pulling out her notebook and opening it to a fresh page.

"There's not much to it," Kelvin said. "I was walking past the gym in the afternoon, and I heard some bouncing sounds. I looked in the door window, but I didn't see anyone. And the lights were off, too. I figured the problem was that I didn't have a good enough view from that window, so I went and got the keys from the main office and opened the door. But no one was in there!"

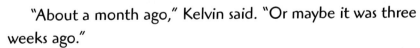

"Wait a second," Ursula said. "When exactly did this happen?"

"About a month ago," Kelvin said. "Or maybe it was three weeks ago."

"Well, which one was it?" Ursula asked, her voice very serious.

"It was probably a month ago," Kelvin said finally. "The *first* time, that is."

"There were *more* times?" Ursula asked with raised eyebrows.

"Yup," Kelvin said. "The same exact thing happened about two weeks ago. Right around the same time in the afternoon."

"What time?" Ursula asked.

"About 4:15," Kelvin said. "The school was pretty empty, so I know it wasn't any earlier than that."

"Did both incidents happen on the same day of the week?" Ursula asked.

"Can't remember," Kelvin said, shaking his head. "I just know they both happened around 4:15."

"Do you know who else was in the building both those times?" I asked.

"I don't know," Kelvin said. "I didn't see anyone anywhere near the gym, at least."

"And no one was in the hall after you came back with the keys?" Ursula asked.

"Nope," Kelvin said.

"And there was nothing left in the gym?" Julian asked.

"Nope," Kelvin said again.

"So you just heard the dribbling and that was it?" Anika asked.

"Yup," Kelvin said. "And by the time I came back, there was no sound at all. It was so strange, like whoever it was had just *vanished.*"

"How long did it take you to get the keys from the main office?" Ursula asked.

"Maybe about a minute," Kelvin said. "No more than that."

"Don't you think the person could've just left when you went to get the keys?" Julian asked.

"I guess so," Kelvin said with a shrug. "That's what Mr. Davidson thought. He thought it was *him*."

"I don't think it was Mr. Davidson," Ursula said suddenly.

Everyone looked at Ursula.

"Why not?" Kelvin asked.

"Well, think about it. Don't you think it's weird that Mr. Davidson would decide to leave exactly when Kelvin went to get the keys, *both times*?"

We all thought about that.

"It's too much of a coincidence," Ursula continued, shaking her head. "I could see that happening *once*, but not twice."

"You're right," I said, and the others nodded.

"Whoever it was didn't want to be seen for some reason, so they must've heard Kelvin coming and made a quick exit," Ursula said, turning to Kelvin and asking: "Could the Dribbler have seen or heard you at the door?"

"Did you make a noise or anything when you peeked through the window?" I added.

"Well, I *did* try to open the door both times, before I realized it was dead-bolted," Kelvin said.

"The Dribbler must've heard *that*," Julian said.

"But how could someone leave the gym, lock the door again, and disappear from the hall while Kelvin was away for *one minute?*" Blitz asked with raised eyebrows.

"The Dribbler could've used the street exit or one of the exits that goes out to the school yard—right, Kelvin?" Ursula asked.

"Well, I checked those doors, but they were all dead-bolted, too," Kelvin said. "And all the outside doors have two sets of locks, so they take a while to open and lock."

"And there's no other way out?" Ursula asked.

"Only the hallway exit we already talked about," Kelvin said. "That's why I thought the whole thing was so strange. I thought my ears were playing tricks on me. I heard the dribbling sound as clear as day, but then when I looked inside, there was no one around!"

"*Spooky*," Blitz said.

"It *was* spooky," Kelvin agreed. "I walk past the gym all the time these days to see if I hear it again. I really want to get to the bottom of this, just for my own peace of mind."

"We'll figure it out," Ursula said confidently. "We specialize in cases like this. We just have to round up as much information as possible."

"*And* we have to hope the Dribbler strikes again," Julian added.

"Exactly," Anika said, and the rest of us agreed.

"Well, I'll let you know if I hear anything more," Kelvin offered.

"And *we'll* keep watch on the gym after school," Ursula said. "We want to be eyewitnesses."

"Or at least *ear* witnesses," Blitz added.

"And *I'll* see what the word is around school," Anika said. "'Cause maybe someone *else* has heard the Dribbler, too."

"Sounds like a plan," I said.

I figured we'd get to the bottom of this one *real* fast. I mean, a *Phantom Dribbler?* You've gotta be kidding me. I couldn't even say that with a straight face. I was sure there was some very simple explanation, and we'd have this operation wrapped up in a couple of days. But little did I know what was in store....

CHAPTER 4

THE MYSTERY DOORS

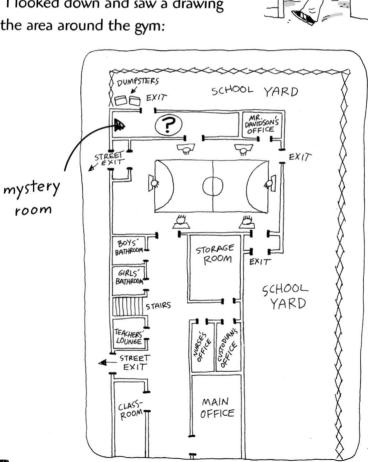

he next morning, I was sitting in homeroom with Julian when Ursula came running in.

"Guys!" she said breathlessly. "I think I'm on to something!"

"What?" Julian and I asked.

"Look!" she said, thrusting her notebook on my desk.

I looked down and saw a drawing of the area around the gym:

"See that mystery room?" Ursula asked, pointing at the room with a question mark on it. "I think *that's* how the Dribbler escaped!"

"Wait—back up a second," I said. "How'd you find out about this *mystery room*?"

"Well," Ursula began, catching her breath, "this morning I decided to draw a map of the area around the gym, because I figured *that* was the best way to start this investigation."

"Lemme guess," I said. "You didn't believe Kelvin when he said there was no other way out of the gym besides the exits he told us about."

"Exactly," Ursula said.

That was Ursula for you—always skeptical until she'd checked the facts herself.

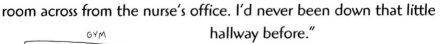

"I was trying to find all the possible escape routes and hiding places the Dribbler could've used," Ursula continued. "So I walked around the halls near the gym and wrote down what the signs on the doors said. I found some rooms that I didn't even know about, like this storage room across from the nurse's office. I'd never been down that little hallway before."

"Did you go inside the gym?" Julian asked.

"I couldn't, 'cause the gym was locked," Ursula explained. "But I *did* peek in the windows. And that's when I saw this door right here that I hadn't ever noticed before."

Ursula pointed at the door to the mystery room on her map. I tried to picture the gym in my mind, but I was drawing a blank on the extra door. I guess I hadn't paid much attention to the gym walls before.

"Oh yeah," Julian said. "I remember that door. It's between those two sets of bleachers."

"Exactly," Ursula said.

door to mystery room

"At first I thought the door went straight outside," Ursula continued, "but then I realized that there had to be another room there, a really long room, or Mr. Davidson's office would stick out into the school yard."

SCHOOL YARD

MR. DAVIDSON'S OFFICE

GYM

NO

SCHOOL YARD

MR. DAVIDSON'S OFFICE

?

GYM

YES

"You're *right*," I said, realizing that Ursula probably *was* on to something.

"And *then* I went outside to see if the mystery room had an outside exit, and sure enough, there was a door near the dumpsters," Ursula said. "I'm *sure* it's an exit from the mystery room."

"Nice work," I said.

"*Now* we just have to get Kelvin to take us into the mystery room today after school, so we can check it out for ourselves and find out what's in there," Ursula said.

"So you think the Dribbler made his escape through there?" Julian asked.

"Yup," Ursula said. "It's perfect. He could walk right out the school-yard gate."

"But why wouldn't Kelvin have *told* us about that room when he was talking about all the exits?" I asked. "He only talked about the hallway exit and the exits that went straight out of the building."

"Yeah," Julian nodded. "He didn't say anything about an exit through another *room*."

Ursula shrugged.

"Guess we'll find out after school," she said. "Or *before* if I can find Kelvin sometime between classes. I can't *wait*."

✳ ✳ ✳ ✳

After lunch that day, the Spy Five met in the school yard. Ursula hadn't had any luck tracking down Kelvin, and Anika hadn't heard about any other reports of mysterious dribbling in the gym after school. But Anika *did* have some interesting news about the old basketball team.

"One of my friends has an older brother who was on the boys' basketball team seven years ago," she began, "and you're never gonna guess what the team was called."

Anika had a huge smile on her face, so I knew the name was bad.

"What?" Julian asked cautiously.

"Well, I guess the way it worked, each school in the basketball league got a color for their uniforms," Anika said, "and the team names always had to do with the colors. Remember the uniforms in the photo we saw?"

"They were gray," Ursula remembered.

"Exactly," Anika said.

"So what was the team called?" Blitz asked.

"Guess," Anika said. "It's something gray."

Everyone thought about it for a second.

"The wolves?" Julian suggested.

"Nice try," Anika said. "But *no.*"

"The skyscrapers?" Ursula offered.

"That would be cool," Anika said. "But this name is *not* cool."

"Give us a hint," Blitz insisted.

"Okay, it's an animal," Anika said, "an animal that lives in New York...in Central Park...in the trees..."

And that's when I realized it. I could hardly believe it.

"The *squirrels?*" I asked.

Anika nodded with a grin.

"OH MAN!" Julian burst out. "You're kidding me. They named their team after TREE RATS?"

"That's DISGUSTING!" Blitz said with a grimace.

"They were the M.S. 1024 Gray Squirrels," Anika said. "They had a mascot in a squirrel costume and everything."

rat   tree rat

"What were they *thinking?*" Julian blasted.

"The name came from a long time ago," Anika said. "I think back then, they had to name the team after an animal that lived in Central Park, and it had to go with the color. Something like that."

"That's *mad* stupid," Julian said.

"They went by 'the Grays' for short, at least," Anika added.

"That's not much better," I said.

"We *have* to come up with a new name for *our* team," Julian said. "'Cause I'm not gonna be a squirrel."

"You *said* it," Anika agreed.

"Yeah," Blitz chimed in. "We could be the Robots! Robots can be gray!"

Everyone was quiet.

"Or wait—how 'bout the *Basketbots*?" Blitz added.

"Um, we have a *long* time to come up with a name," Anika said diplomatically. "But we can keep those options in mind."

And then suddenly Ursula had one of her outbursts:

"ANOTHER DOOR!" she shouted, pointing across the school yard.

We all turned and looked at the door she was pointing at. It was near one of the gym exits. It didn't *look* like the gym exit doors, though. It was just a single door (not a pair of double doors), and it didn't even have a handle, just a lock on the side. We all went over to get a closer look at it.

Ursula pulled out her notebook and looked at her sketch of the building layout.

"I bet this door connects to the storage room across from the custodian's office!" Ursula said, quickly correcting her sketch.

"And maybe the storage room connects to the gym!" I said, pointing to the wall the storage room shared with the gym.

"Exactly!" Ursula said, adding a possible door connecting the gym with the storage room.

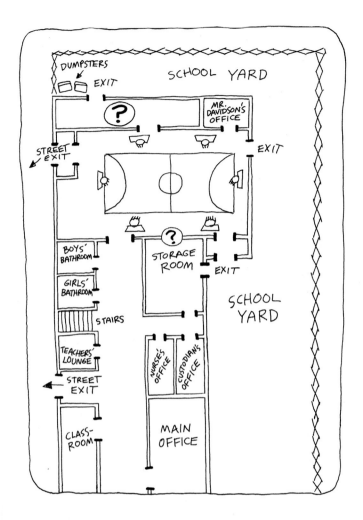

"All these extra doors!" Anika marveled. "I never noticed them before."

"Me neither," I agreed, and the others nodded, too.

"I'm *sure* they're the key to cracking this case," Ursula said. "I bet you a million bucks."

I guess everyone else was pretty sure, too, because no one took Ursula up on her bet.

That day after school, we all went racing around to find Kelvin. Lucky for us, this time we found him standing in the hall right outside the gym with his mop bucket.

"Kelvin!" Ursula called from all the way down the hall. "*There* you are!"

> KELVIN!

And we all ran up to him.

"What's all the excitement about?" Kelvin asked, looking alarmed.

"We want to see what's inside this door!" Ursula said, showing her sketch of the building to Kelvin. "And we want to see if there's a door *here*!"

Kelvin squinted at Ursula's sketch, looking puzzled.

"We're trying to figure out the Dribbler's escape route," I explained.

"*Oh*, I see," Kelvin said. "You kids sure work fast!"

"This case is our top priority," Ursula said in a very serious tone.

"Well, I'm going to need my reading glasses so I can look at your picture," Kelvin said, fumbling in his pockets.

"Can we go inside the gym and see for ourselves?" Ursula asked urgently. "PLEASE?"

"Well, sure," Kelvin said. "I actually have the keys already, because I was going to head in there next."

So we all followed behind as Kelvin opened the gym door. Ursula immediately ran inside.

"LOOK!" she said, pointing at an unmarked door on the wall that the gym shared with the storage room. "There IS a door there!"

"Does that door go to the storage room?" I asked Kelvin.

"The *storage* room?" Kelvin asked. "That's a *locker* room."

"A LOCKER ROOM?!" we all repeated.

"The *boys'* locker room," Kelvin clarified.

"And that must be the *girls'* locker room," I said, pointing across the gym at the door between the bleachers that Ursula had spotted that morning.

"Yup," Kelvin said.

"We have *locker rooms?*" Blitz asked. "How come we don't use them?"

"Guess there's no need for them," Kelvin said with a shrug.

"We don't have any sports teams, and we don't change clothes for gym," Anika pointed out.

"I don't think those locker rooms have been used for six years," Kelvin said. "That's when the school had a basketball team. But then the coach...um..."

"We *know*," Ursula interrupted.

"It happened right around this time of year, actually. It was very sad," Kelvin continued. "You know, he used to play basketball in here every day after school."

"He *did?*" Blitz asked, his eyes wide.

"Yes," Kelvin said. "That's why it was so strange to hear the dribbling again—and then find no one in here."

"You don't think it was his *ghost*, do you?" Ursula asked.

"Well, I don't think so," Kelvin said. "Because I don't really believe in that stuff. But I have to say, it *did* cross my mind."

"There's gotta be a logical explanation," I said.

"And *that's* what we're going to find," Ursula said firmly.

"So can we open up the locker rooms and look inside?" I asked.

"Oh, I don't have the keys to those doors," Kelvin said. "Maybe Mr. Davidson does?"

"But he's already gone for the day," Blitz said, pointing at Mr. Davidson's closed office door. Mr. Davidson pretty much always left around 2:45, right after school ended.

"Can't we check in the main office?" Ursula suggested. "Maybe the keys are there?"

"I suppose we could check," Kelvin said.

So we all headed to the main office. Ursula drilled Kelvin with questions as we walked.

"Let me get this straight," Ursula said. "I want to make sure my map of the building is exactly right. So there's a storage room next to the locker room?"

SO THERE'S A STORAGE ROOM NEXT TO THE LOCKER ROOM?

IS IT CONNECTED TO THE LOCKER ROOM?

WHO HAS KEYS TO IT?

AND, WHAT'S STORED THERE?

"There is," Kelvin confirmed.

"Is it *connected* to the locker room?" Ursula asked.

"I don't think so," Kelvin said. "But I don't use that storage room, so I can't tell you for sure."

"Can we check?"

"I suppose."

"Who has keys to it?" Ursula asked. "And what's stored there?"

"So many questions!" Kelvin said, looking at Ursula with wide eyes.

"Well, how else do you expect to get answers?" Ursula asked.

At that point, we were already at the main office. Mrs. Spicer, the school secretary, wasn't at her desk, and Mr. Naulty's office door was closed.

"Do you think Mr. Naulty's in there?" Blitz asked nervously.

"Doubt it," Kelvin said. "I've seen him leaving early these days. He always gets like that toward the end of the year."

Kelvin took us straight to the back of the office where there was a big cabinet full of keys. He opened it up.

"Let's have a look here," Kelvin said. "Does anyone see any labels that say 'locker room'?"

We all scanned the labels below the keys. I saw labels that said "Book Closet #2" and "Kitchen" and "Nurse's Office," but they weren't in any kind of order. And there were a *ton* of them. It looked like it was going to take a while to search. But unfortunately, we didn't *have* a while, because we were suddenly interrupted by...

MR. NAULTY!

He threw open his office door and stepped out with his usual ferocious face.

"EXCUSE ME!" he blasted. "Students are NOT ALLOWED in the key cabinet!"

"Sorry!" Kelvin said quickly. "We were just leaving."

"You kids should not even be in the *building*!" Mr. Naulty kept blasting. "It's time to GO HOME!"

"We're *leaving*," Julian said with a scowl.

And with that, the five of us scooted out of the office. Kelvin stayed behind to lock up the key cabinet and, I'm sure, get more of an earful from Mr. Naulty.

"Leave it to Mr. *Naulty* to ruin the investigation," Blitz complained as we all walked out of the building.

"It's just a minor setback," Ursula said, pulling out her notebook again. "Our map of the gym area is getting more and more complete. And tomorrow, we'll be *back*."

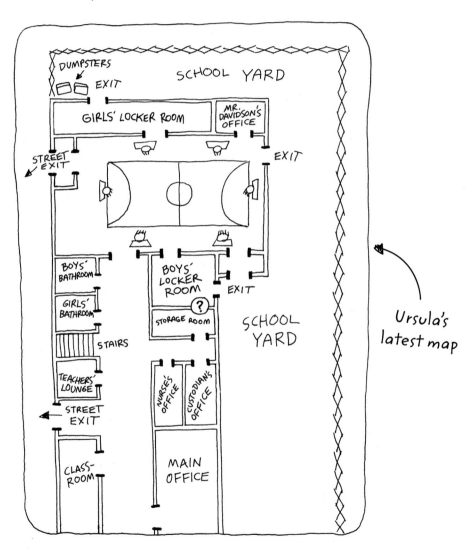

Ursula's latest map

CHAPTER 6
URSULA'S CLOSE ONE

The next day, we set up a schedule for patrolling the gym after school. Since Ursula and Blitz lived really near the school, they could both arrange to be there sometime between 4 and 4:30 pretty much every day. Julian and I were able to be there most of the time, too, and Anika managed to stop by some days on her way home from dance class. We were totally determined to catch the Dribbler in the act.

But you know what? After four days of gym-patrolling, we'd *still* never heard the Dribbler. Not one single, solitary dribble.

And Kelvin hadn't heard any more dribbling, either.

We were all starting to wonder if Kelvin's ears really *had* played tricks on him. But Kelvin was sticking to his story.

I KNOW I HEARD DRIBBLING! **TWICE!**

Then Kelvin found out something *else* that raised our eyebrows: The locker room keys were missing from their hook in the key cabinet! Kelvin said he'd checked the cabinet several days in a row, but the keys never came back.

We asked Mr. Davidson if *he* had keys to the locker rooms, but he said he didn't have any of his own, and that the only keys he knew of were the ones in the main office. (And then, of course, Mr. Davidson asked why we were asking, so we had to tell him we were investigating the Dribbler. He said he thought we were wasting our time, but we didn't let *that* stop us.)

Anyway, after we'd established that the locker room keys were missing in action, Ursula became convinced that the Dribbler was using one of the locker room exits and leaving through the school-yard gate. Seemed like a pretty solid theory to me.

I just wished the Dribbler would hurry up and strike again. 'Cause I for one was getting a little tired of waiting.

✷ ✷ ✷ ✷

My wish came true about a week after we started our Dribbler investigation. It was a Wednesday, and all five of us were at school, hanging out in the library. We decided to swing by the gym at about 4:10.

We didn't hear anything as we walked toward the gym, even when we got right up to the doors. But just as we were about to turn around, we heard the first dribble.

"Wait!" Ursula said.

And then we heard *another* dribble. And then a whole bunch of 'em, loud and clear.

Immediately we all tried to jam our faces up in the gym door windows, but the windows were really small, so we couldn't see the whole gym. Plus, the windows were really high up, so it was hard to get a good look in there. *And* they were covered in about twenty years' worth of nose grease, so they were murky as anything.

"Whaddya see? Whaddya see?" Blitz kept asking, because he was too short to look for himself.

"*Nothing,*" Julian said with a scowl, trying to plaster his face against the window to get a better angle.

"The Dribbler must be using the hoop way down at the far end," Ursula said. "That's why we can't see him...or *her.*"

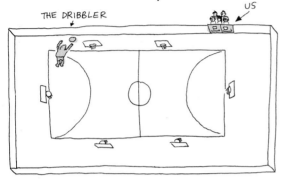

Then, suddenly, right after Ursula spoke, the dribbling stopped! It was as if the Dribbler had heard something and was listening for more. Anika put her finger up to her lips, and we all waited in silence, looking at each other with wide eyes.

As the seconds of silence ticked sloooowly by, I listened carefully for sounds of footsteps or doors, because I was afraid the Dribbler would slip out of the gym before we had a chance to make the catch.

But then finally, just when I was starting to think we'd totally blown it, the dribbling started again. *Phew!*

"Let's spread out and cover all the exits," Ursula whispered, quickly opening her notebook to her map page.

"I'll take the street exit," Anika volunteered.

"And we'll cover the school yard," Julian said quietly, motioning to me and Blitz.

"And *I'll* stay here," Ursula said, looking as intense as ever. "This is *it,* guys!"

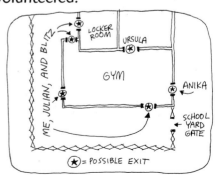

"Let's go!" Blitz whispered excitedly.

So Blitz, Julian, and I raced down to the cafeteria and out the door to the school yard.

It was roasting hot outside, even though it was late in the afternoon, and my eyes hurt from the bright light. But still, we all charged across the school yard to the gym.

None of the gym windows were at ground level, so we couldn't peek inside them. And we couldn't *hear* the dribbling, since all the windows were closed.

"Let's see if we can hear through the doors," I suggested, running up to the gym doors (which were locked) and pressing my ear against them.

Julian and Blitz ran up beside me and pressed their ears against the doors, too. And sure enough, we could just barely make out the sound of the bouncing ball inside. So it was confirmed—the Dribbler was still in there. Now it was just a matter of waiting him (or *her*) out.

So we stepped back and stood in the middle of the school yard, where we could see all of the exits the Dribbler might use.

But before we'd waited too long, Julian got an idea.

"Let's go check with Anika," he said, pointing to the school-yard gate, since the exit Anika was watching was just on the other side of it. "The door over there has windows on it, so maybe she can look inside!"

"Yeah!" Blitz agreed.

"I'll wait here," I offered, since I didn't want to risk missing the Dribbler's exit.

So Blitz and Julian ran over to the school-yard gate and called to Anika. She quickly came over to the fence, and I could see her shake her head. No luck.

Blitz and Julian came running back to me right after that.

"Anika said she couldn't see through to the gym, because the second set of doors on the *inside* were closed," Blitz reported.

"Too bad," I said.

"*Annoying*," Julian said with a scowl. "I bet the Dribbler closed them just so people couldn't see in."

"Hey, *I* know!" Blitz said suddenly. "You guys can lift me up so I can look in *there*!"

Blitz was pointing at one of the big gym windows that was about seven or eight feet off the ground.

"You think we can lift you all the way up *there*?" Julian asked, eyeing the height.

"I can stand on your hands!" Blitz said, cupping his hands together to demonstrate. "Like this!"

"Guess it's worth a try," I said.

So Blitz stood between me and Julian and stepped on our hands, first mine, then Julian's. Let me tell you, he was heavier than he looked!

"Higher, guys!" Blitz said in a loud whisper.

"We're *trying*!" Julian grunted.

After a couple of false starts, Julian and I managed to lift Blitz high enough so he could grab the ledge and pull himself up to peek in the bottom of the window, just barely.

"I can see!" Blitz said excitedly. "I can see!"

Then he got real quiet.

"What do you see?" I whispered.

Blitz was still quiet, and his mouth was hanging open.

"*Nothing*," Blitz said finally. "No one's in there!"

Julian and I immediately lowered Blitz to the ground.

"Are you SURE?" Julian demanded.

Blitz nodded with wide eyes.

"I saw the whole gym, and there was NOBODY!"

I ran over to the gym door and pressed my ear to it again. Julian and Blitz followed and listened, too.

Nothing.

"Maybe the Dribbler went in the locker room," I suggested.

"Or out one of the other doors!" Blitz added. "Like Ursula's door!"

"Or maybe *Anika* saw something," Julian said, taking off toward the school-yard gate.

It seemed like everyone was in a panic.

"Let's go see Ursula!" Blitz said to me.

"Hold on, guys," I said, trying to decide on the best plan. "The Dribbler might still be in the locker room..."

But Blitz was already off and running toward the school entrance. I decided to go ahead and follow Blitz, since Julian and Anika would have the outside exits covered.

So, Blitz and I dashed through the cafeteria, up the stairs, and down the hall toward the gym. And as we were coming down the home stretch, we saw a very strange sight...

URSULA'S FEET!

It looked like Ursula was lying on the floor of the short hallway that went back to the nurse's office and the storage room. Her feet were sticking out into the main hall, and that's all we could see. Blitz and I looked at each other in shock.

"URSULA!" Blitz shouted, totally freaking out. "ARE YOU OKAY?"

And suddenly Ursula's feet were whipped out of sight and the other half of her body came into view.

"SHHH!" she whispered harshly.

But it was too late. We'd been heard.

Out of the main office stepped Mrs. Spicer, looking VERY ALARMED.

"Are you children all right?" she asked, putting her hand over her mouth in horror when she saw Ursula on the floor.

"Oh, I'm okay!" Ursula said, quickly standing up.

"My heart is just *pounding*!" Mrs. Spicer said, taking a deep breath. "What is going on here?"

But before we could even *begin* to answer, we heard...

And out stepped Mr. Naulty himself.

We all cringed. Busted!

But Mr. Naulty didn't even *wait* for us to answer the question he claimed he was going to ask. He just kept blasting away. He was so mad, his face was the color of a lobster.

"You are NOT PERMITTED to be RUNNING WILD around the school hallways AFTER SCHOOL HOURS," Mr. Naulty said. "In fact, you're not permitted to be here AT ALL unless you are IN A CLASSROOM, WITH A TEACHER."

We all looked at the floor.

"We're allowed to be in the *library*," Ursula dared to say.

Blitz and I winced. I think Mrs. Spicer did, too.

"IS THIS THE LIBRARY?" Mr. Naulty blasted.

"I didn't mean—" Ursula started to say.

"IS THIS THE LIBRARY?" Mr. Naulty blasted again.

"NO," Blitz and I chimed in, trying to help Ursula out.

"That's what I thought," Mr. Naulty said. "And didn't I see you kids here after school *last* week, digging through the key cabinet?"

Ooh! *Double* busted! All of us were speechless.

"That's ALSO what I thought," Mr. Naulty said. "We have rules at this school that are for YOUR OWN SAFETY. If I see any of you wandering the halls unsupervised again, I will call ALL OF YOUR PARENTS. Is that understood?"

We all looked at the floor and nodded. Ursula didn't even *try* to debate again. Personally, *I* had a bone to pick with Mr. Naulty and his so-called *rules*, because half the time people didn't follow them and nothing ever happened to them. But of course I wasn't about to make things worse than they already were.

"All right, it's time to go home. All of you, right now. Let's go," Mr. Naulty barked, pointing down the hall toward the main exit.

So we all started walking out in silence.

And that's when I looked up and saw Anika and Julian swing around the corner. They saw us right away and screeched to a halt, but it was too late. Mr. Naulty had already seen them.

SCREECH!

"ALL OF YOU, OUT!" Mr. Naulty blasted down the hall. "IMMEDIATELY!"

"*Okay, okay*," Julian and Anika said, turning around and heading back out.

When Blitz, Ursula, and I finally got outside, Julian and Anika came running up to us with wide eyes.

"What *happened*?" they both demanded.

"Ursula was flat on the floor!" Blitz said, looking totally flustered.

"Why were you on the *floor*?!" Anika asked Ursula.

"I heard doors close!" Ursula said. "*Two* doors!"

"AND YOU FELL ON THE FLOOR?" Blitz blasted.

"I was trying to look *under* the doors!" Ursula said.

"You looked like you were DEAD!" Blitz insisted.

"What, you thought I got *dribbled* to death?" Ursula shot back.

"*People!*" I said, trying to put a stop to the madness. "Can we get back to the point? Did anyone see the Dribbler?"

"NO," everyone said.

"I *almost* did!" Ursula said. "I was so close, I could kill myself!"

Ursula looked like she was in actual pain.

"What happened?" I asked.

"Well, the dribbling stopped, and I just stood there in the hallway, waiting and waiting for it to start again, like before. The whole time, I didn't take my eye off the girls' locker room door on the other side of the gym, in case the Dribbler left through there. But I never saw anything. And then the next thing I knew, I heard a door close behind me, down that little hallway where the nurse's office is. I thought it was the nurse or somebody. But then I heard a key unlocking *another* door, and I put two and two together."

"You mean you think the storage room IS connected to the boys' locker room?" I asked.

"Exactly!" Ursula said. "The Dribbler slipped right out through there and then went inside one of the offices down that little hallway—the nurse's office or the head custodian's office!"

"So you think it was the nurse or the head custodian?" Julian asked.

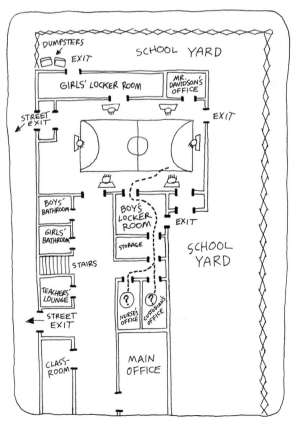

We all pictured both those people. Not likely suspects. Mr. Raymond, the head custodian (Kelvin's boss), didn't exactly look like an athlete. And the nurse, Ms. Muller, didn't either—she looked like she'd get blown over by a strong breeze. Neither of them seemed like Phantom Dribbler material.

Mr. Raymond, the head custodian

Ms. Muller, the nurse

"Well, it *could* be one of them. Or maybe it's just someone who has *keys* to one of their offices," Ursula said. "I don't know. I just know I missed the whole thing!"

"So the Dribbler was in one of those offices when we were getting bawled out by Mr. Naulty?"

"I *think* so, but I don't know," Ursula said with a shrug. "All I know is if I had just walked down the hall and looked when I heard the first door close, the case would be cracked! UGH! I could murder myself!"

Ursula stomped her foot so hard, it was like she was trying to dent the sidewalk.

"Come on," Anika said, trying to make Ursula feel better, "you couldn't have known about the storage room being connected."

"Yeah I could've! Remember when I asked Kelvin to open up the storage room? Well, he never did, and I should've kept trying so we could've seen for ourselves if there was a door to the locker room!" Ursula said, scrunching up her face in frustration. "I can't believe I dropped the ball like that! I usually chase down EVERY LEAD!"

That was true.

"Give yourself a break," Anika said. "We'll get another chance."

"No, we won't," Ursula wailed. "Mr. Naulty totally busted us!"

"But tomorrow's another day!" Anika said. "Remember you said that before?"

"Not *this* time," Ursula said. "Mr. Naulty said he'd call our parents if he caught us walking around the halls after school again."

"HE DID?" Julian asked.

"Yup," I said.

"But people *always* walk around the halls after school," Julian argued.

"*Tell* me about it," I said. "But *we* got busted, so now *we* can't."

"So it's a lost cause," Ursula said. "How are we supposed to investigate if we can't walk around the halls after school? We have to be able to walk past the gym to see what's going on in there, at least a couple of times a day..."

And that's when Blitz, who'd been quiet for a while, suddenly spoke up.

"Actually," he said, "I think there might be a way we can keep the investigation going."

"Really?" I asked. "How?"

"Well," Blitz said, "it's kinda hard to explain, but if you want to come to my place, I can show you something pretty cool."

And of course, Blitz didn't have to say another word. We were all immediately on our way over there.

CHAPTER 7
AN ALARMING IDEA

When we got to Blitz's place, Blitz went into his closet, dug around for a while, and finally came out with a shoe box.

Blitz opened the box and pulled out a little pyramid.

"What's *that* do?" Julian asked.

"It's a perimeter alarm," Blitz explained. "Watch."

Blitz sat the pyramid on his desk and switched it on.

"Wait three seconds for it to get ready," Blitz said to Julian, "then walk in front of it."

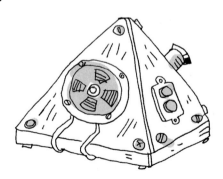

So, after three seconds, Julian stepped in front of the pyramid, and the thing started blaring.

"Sweet!" Julian said.

"How's it work?" I asked.

"It detects changes in the light when you walk in front of the sensor," Blitz explained, pointing to the tube sticking out of the pyramid. "When the light changes, the alarm sounds. Really simple."

"And you think we can use *that* to catch the Dribbler?" Anika asked.

"Yeah," Blitz said. "I was thinking we could use it to find out when the Dribbler goes into the gym. Then we could head right down there to catch him!"

"Wait, back up a second. *How* do you want to use the alarm?" Ursula asked.

"Well, we could stick it in the window at the end of that little hallway where the Dribbler came out," Blitz explained. "You gotta figure the Dribbler goes *into* the gym the same way. So he'll walk right by the alarm and set it off!"

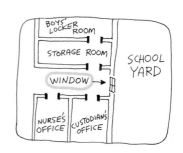

Ursula opened her notebook and looked at her sketch.

"You mean the little window down *there*?" she asked. "It *opens*?"

"Yeah," Blitz said. "When Mr. Naulty was yelling at us, I looked over there, and I noticed it was open. That got me thinking. I figured we could put the alarm on the outside ledge and stick the nozzle through the open part of the window. Then we could wait out in the school yard till we heard the alarm—"

"We're not technically supposed to be hanging around out *there*, either," Ursula interrupted. "We could get busted for that, too."

"Yeah," I nodded. "That's why they lock the gate after school."

But Blitz was not defeated.

"No problem," he said. "We can wait in any room that has a window on the school-yard side of the building. As long as the window's open, we'll hear the alarm."

"We could wait in the library!" Ursula said excitedly.

"Exactly," Blitz said. "The library's perfect, actually, 'cause it's practically right upstairs from the window with the alarm. We could just hang out in the library as long as we needed to, and then when we heard the alarm, we could go down to the school yard and take a peek inside the gym. That way we wouldn't have to be down there more than a couple of minutes. Not much chance of getting busted—"

"But how would we see into the gym?" Julian asked.

"Easy," Blitz said. "We can use a ladder to look in the window. We're gonna need a ladder anyway to set up the alarm. So we'd just leave it out there—"

"Where would we get a *ladder?*" Ursula interrupted.

"I'm sure Kelvin has one," Blitz said. "And if not, my dad has one downstairs in our storage room. I'd just sneak it into the school yard after school, before they lock the gates."

Everyone considered that.

"Okay," Julian said. "Sounds like it could work."

"Yeah," the girls agreed.

But *I* wasn't convinced.

"But guys," I said, "the Dribbler isn't the *only* person who uses that hallway. The head custodian and the nurse have offices there."

Blitz thought for a second.

"We could have an advance team that goes down first to check out every alarm," he said. "And if it's a false alarm, they could just reset the device. If it's the real deal, they could signal to everyone else from the school yard."

"Yeah!" Julian agreed. "*I'll* be on the advance team."

"Okay, that could work," I said, "but there's still another thing: If the alarm's loud enough for *us* to hear, the Dribbler will hear it, too. That could ruin everything. You know, the Dribbler could realize something was up and decide not to risk getting caught."

Everyone got quiet.

"*I* was thinking of that, too," Blitz said, "and I was thinking I could change the alarm so it was the kind of sound you hear outside all the time. You know, something ordinary so the Dribbler wouldn't notice it. I have lots of different sounds I could swap in, like a dog barking, or a plane flying overhead, or birds chirping...or something like that."

chirping alarm   barking alarm   motorcycle alarm

"But then would *we* be able to hear it?" Ursula asked.

Blitz thought about that one.

"Guess we'd have to test out lots of options," Blitz said finally, "and I'll think about it some more. I'm positive I can make this work *somehow*."

"*I'm* positive, too," Anika said.

"Yeah," the rest of us agreed.

And so the investigation was up and running again!

CHAPTER 8
THE DRIBBLER'S PERSONAL STINK

T he next morning at school, Blitz came running up to me and Julian in the hall. He looked really excited.

"A thirty-second delay!" he shouted.

A THIRTY-SECOND DELAY!

"*What?*" Julian and I both asked.

"A thirty-second delay!" Blitz said again. "I'll set up the alarm so there's thirty seconds of silence before the alarm sounds. Then the Dribbler will be out of the hallway already!"

"Nice!" I said.

"*And* I gave it a cool sound, too," Blitz said, and he pulled out the alarm, flipped it on, and waved his hand in front of it.

Nothing happened.

"We have to wait thirty seconds, of course," Blitz explained. "I'll head down to the end of the hall so we can make sure it's loud enough."

So Blitz ran down the hall and, to our surprise, the alarm started *giggling.*

"It's my little sister's laugh," Blitz said. "It's the kind of sound that'll blend in for everyone else, but *I'll* recognize it right away."

"Perfect!" Julian said.

Leave it to Blitz to think of something like that.

✻ ✻ ✻

That day at lunch, Blitz showed the girls his giggling alarm, and we checked out the window where we were planning to put it.

"I can come down here and set the thing up at about 3:00 or so," Blitz said. "Then we can all just wait in the library till the Dribbler makes an appearance."

"*If* he comes today," I added, considering we'd waited a whole week for the first appearance.

"What makes you so sure it's a *he?*" Ursula asked me. "*I* think it's the nurse."

"Really?" Anika asked with raised eyebrows. "Why?"

"Well, she wears sneakers *every* day," Ursula said.

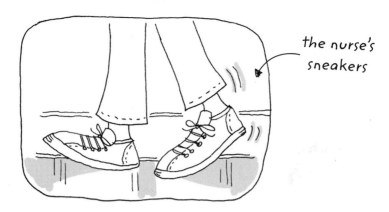

the nurse's sneakers

"Don't *all* nurses wear sneakers?" Blitz asked. "Isn't that, like, part of their nurse uniform?"

"Yeah," Julian agreed.

"Well, *I* think it's a good theory, since she has an office in the right place, *and* she has the right shoes," Ursula said with a shrug. "And I wouldn't guess the head custodian, since he looks like he hasn't exercised in about five hundred years. And does anyone else have a *better* suspect?"

Everyone was quiet. I knew *I* didn't have any suspects in mind. I just figured it was one of the teachers, one I'd never met before, like an eighth-grade teacher or something.

"*I* think we should talk to the nurse and the head custodian," Anika said. "'Cause even if it's not one of them, they could've seen something. They're our best possible witnesses."

"True," I said.

"Maybe we can stop by their offices right after school ends, before the halls clear out, so we don't get in trouble again," Anika said.

"Good plan," I said.

So we all agreed that we'd meet in the library right after school and head downstairs together.

But then something *huge* happened that afternoon. Ursula, Julian, and I had gym last period that day, and Mr. Davidson had a big surprise for us after class.

"Guess what I found," Mr. Davidson said.

"What?" we all asked.

"The keys to the locker rooms!" Mr. Davidson said, holding up a set of keys on a long string. "Found 'em hanging on a hook in my closet. They were Mr. Camacho's spare keys."

Ursula, Julian, and I stepped back a little. It still kind of freaked me out to look at Mr. Camacho's old stuff.

"I thought we could all take a peek inside the locker rooms, since you were so curious," Mr. Davidson said. "And now's the perfect time, unless you have somewhere you have to be after school. I have about ten minutes before I have to leave."

"Let's go now!" Ursula said excitedly.

"What about Anika and Blitz?" Julian asked, since we were supposed to meet them in the library right after school.

"We can meet them *later*," Ursula said. "Let's go!"

So we all headed across the gym to the boys' locker room.

"I have to admit, you got me curious when you told me the locker room keys were missing from the main office," Mr. Davidson said as we walked over to the door. "Made me wonder if there really *is* someone sneaking in here after school."

"Oh, there *is*," Ursula said firmly. "We heard the dribbling with our *own* ears yesterday at about 4:00."

"You *did?*" Mr. Davidson asked.

We all nodded.

"But we couldn't see who it was," Ursula said. "We couldn't see *anything* through the door windows."

"It wasn't *you*, was it?" I asked Mr. Davidson, just to be sure.

"Nope," Mr. Davidson said. "I'm out of here by 2:30 on Wednesdays."

When Mr. Davidson said *that*, I started to wonder if maybe the Dribbler knew Mr. Davidson's schedule. But before I could think much more about that, Mr. Davidson swung open the boys' locker room door, and we all stepped inside.

Mr. Davidson flipped on the ceiling lights, but most of them didn't work, so it was really gloomy in there. And it smelled like a mixture of dust and old sweat.

"*Ugh*," Ursula said. "This place has been out of use for six years, and it *still* smells like an armpit."

Suddenly Julian stopped dead in his tracks.

"Um...maybe it's *not* so out-of-use," Julian said, pointing at one of the lockers.

We all looked where Julian was pointing, and to our shock, we saw...

AN OPEN LOCKER FULL OF STUFF!

"You think it's the *Dribbler's* stuff?" I asked Ursula and Julian.

"That's *my* bet," Ursula said, rushing toward the locker with Julian.

"Check out these shoes!" Julian said, picking one of them up. "Aw, man! They smell *nasty!*"

"So *that's* what's polluting the air in here," Ursula said, waving her hand in front of her nose.

Mr. Davidson looked at the shoe.

"Pretty big," he said, checking the label inside. "Men's size twelve. Wonder whose they could be."

"Guess they're *not* the nurse's!" Julian said to Ursula.

"It was just a *theory*," Ursula said defensively.

Then Julian reached back inside the locker and pulled out the shirt that was hanging on the hook.

"Man," he said, holding up the shirt. "This thing stinks, too."

"*Ew,*" Ursula said. "Hasn't the Dribbler ever heard of *washing his clothes?*"

I touched the shirt, and it was stiff and crunchy from dried sweat.

"You don't think this stuff could've been left in here six years ago, do you?" I asked Mr. Davidson.

"I don't think so," Mr. Davidson said. "I came in here a few times last year, and I never noticed this stuff. I wonder whose it could be..."

"Someone *big*," Ursula said.

"Yeah, *big*," Julian said, holding up a huge pair of blue shorts.

"And there's nothing in the pockets?" Mr. Davidson asked.

"Nope," Julian said.

The last thing in the locker was a pair of white tube socks, lying in the bottom of the locker like a pair of dead fish. Nobody wanted to go *near* those.

"We should put everything back exactly like we found it," Ursula said. "We don't want the Dribbler to know we're on to him."

Then Ursula quickly turned around and started running toward the far end of the locker room.

"*Whoa*, hold on. Where are you going?" Mr. Davidson asked.

"I'm looking for the storage room door," Ursula called back. "The Dribbler's way out!"

"*What?*" Mr. Davidson asked.

"That's how the Dribbler got out yesterday," I explained quickly as Julian put the Dribbler's stuff back into the locker.

"We want to retrace his steps!" Ursula added.

"Wait, how do you—" Mr. Davidson started to ask, but before he could finish, Julian and I took off to find Ursula.

Sure enough, Ursula had found the door to the storage room, and it was unlocked.

"So the Dribbler changes his clothes back there and leaves them in his locker," Ursula said, "and then he goes out *this* door to the storage room..."

Julian and I followed Ursula into the storage room, which was piled high with boxes of paper for the copy machine and other school supplies.

"And then the Dribbler goes out *this* door," Ursula said, pulling open the storage room door and stepping out into the hallway. "And he ends up here. And *then* the question is, where does he go from here?"

And then suddenly a big idea dawned on me.

"Can I see that map you made of the school?" I asked Ursula.

"Sure," she said, pulling her notebook out of her backpack and opening it to her map page.

"You know how you realized there was a link between the storage room and the locker room?" I asked Ursula.

"Yeah," Ursula said.

"I think there's *another* missing link in this map," I said. "And I think *that's* the key to the Dribbler's escape."

"Wait," Ursula said, grabbing the map back. "Let *me* figure it out!"

Ursula looked down at the map, and Julian

crowded beside her so he could look, too. Right then, Mr. Davidson stepped out of the storage room door.

"I had no idea this storage room was connected to the locker room," Mr. Davidson said. "How strange."

"I bet most people at this school don't know about it," I said. "Probably only a select few..."

Ursula and Julian suddenly looked up from the map.

"I got it!" Ursula said.

"Me too!" Julian said.

"You got *what?*" Mr. Davidson asked, looking down at the map.

"The Dribbler's escape route!" Ursula said.

And I knew who the Dribbler was, too. I just knew it in my gut. All the pieces were falling into place. And I could tell by the looks on Julian and Ursula's faces that they had come to the same crazy conclusion.

"Are you guys thinking what *I'm* thinking?" Ursula asked.

"You think it's...*him?*" Julian asked with a wrinkled nose.

Ursula and I both nodded with wide eyes.

Now it was just a matter of proving it....

"**M**r. Davidson," Ursula said urgently, "does the nurse's office or the custodian's office go through to the main office?"

"I think the custodian's office does," Mr. Davidson said.

"You *think* or you *know*?" Ursula demanded.

Mr. Davidson looked taken aback.

"Lemme get this straight," Mr. Davidson said. "You think this Dribbler person goes from the locker room, *through* the storage room, *through* the custodian's office, to the main office?"

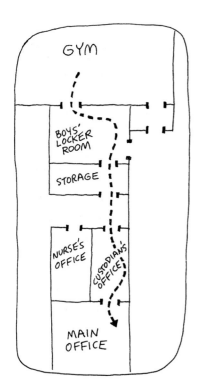

"Exactly," I said. "We just need to know if that last part is really possible."

"Well, I haven't paid *that* much attention to the way the main office is set up, and there are quite a few office doors in there, but I'm pretty sure one of them is the custodian's."

"So that must be it!" Ursula said. "That's the route!"

"But why would someone take such a long route through so many rooms?" Mr. Davidson asked. "Why not just walk through the hall like everyone else?"

"*Because—*" Ursula started to explain.

But before Ursula could finish, we heard footsteps coming down the hall, and we all turned to see...

ANIKA AND BLITZ!

"*There* you are!" Anika said.

"What are you doing *here*?" Blitz asked. "We were supposed to meet in the library! *Then* we were gonna come down here. That was the *plan!*"

"We were in the locker room!" Ursula explained. "We saw the Dribbler's stuff!"

"**YOU DID?!**" Blitz and Anika said at once, really loud.

"*And* we figured out that this office connects to the main office!" Ursula said, tapping on the custodian's door.

"**IT DOES?**" Anika and Blitz shot back.

"Yes!" Ursula said. "*And* we think we know who the Dribbler—"

And then, suddenly, to our horror, the custodian's door swung open!

Ursula stopped mid-sentence, and we all watched to see who would come out...

To our relief, it was just the head custodian, Mr. Raymond. *Phew!*

"What's all this commotion here?" he asked.

I quickly peeked into Mr. Raymond's office, and I saw just what I expected to see: a door on the other side. It was even open, and I could see into the main office.

"Mr. Raymond," I asked, as politely as possible. "We were just wondering: Does anyone walk through your office to get to this hallway?"

"Sure," Mr. Raymond said, "from time to time, people come through here. I don't mind. Mrs. Spicer sometimes comes through here to get to the storage room..."

"See?" Ursula said, looking at Anika and Blitz like her point was proven. "Just like we thought."

"You thought it was *Mrs. Spicer?*" Blitz asked, looking at Ursula like she was insane.

I had to laugh at the thought of Mrs. Spicer shooting hoops.

"No, *not* Mrs. Spicer! I just meant that people *do* cut through Mr. Raymond's office, just like we thought," Ursula explained. "Like I'm sure *Mr. Naulty* does."

"Oh yes," Mr. Raymond said, "he comes through here sometimes on his way to the restroom over there."

"Exactly," Ursula said, looking very pleased, turning to Blitz and Anika. "There's your Dribbler."

"MR. NAULTY IS THE DRIBBLER?!" Anika and Blitz blasted.

"Guys," I said, holding my fingers to my lips, because Mr. Naulty's office wasn't *that* far away. "Shhh!"

"The *Dribbler*?" Mr. Raymond asked, looking confused.

"He plays basketball in the gym after school," Julian explained.

"Mr. *Naulty*?" Mr. Davidson repeated.

And then suddenly we heard:

"Are you looking for me?"

And we looked up to see Mrs. Spicer peeking through the open doorway on the other side of Mr. Raymond's office.

"I thought I heard my name just now," she explained. "Do you need me for something?"

"Um, no," I said. "Sorry to bother you."

"Are you looking for Mr. Naulty?" she asked.

"**NO!**" everyone blurted out at once.

"Well, good," Mrs. Spicer said. "Because he's already gone for the day."

Phew! I was glad to hear *that*. And since the coast was clear, I figured I might as well ask Mrs. Spicer some questions.

"Mrs. Spicer," I began. "Did you know that Mr. Naulty plays *basketball*?"

Mrs. Spicer looked surprised.

"Well, of course," she said. "He used to be quite a basketball star in his youth, you know."

HE USED TO BE QUITE A BASKETBALL STAR IN HIS YOUTH, YOU KNOW.

"**HE DID?**" we all said in shock.

"Yes," Mrs. Spicer nodded. "He almost became a professional basketball player."

"**FOR REAL?**" Julian asked.

"Yes," Mrs. Spicer nodded matter-of-factly.

"I had no idea," Mr. Davidson said. "I wonder why he never told me. We even talked about starting a basketball team, and he never mentioned anything!"

"Well," Mrs. Spicer said with a wince. "I think he's a bit embarrassed about being so...um...out of shape. He used to be a very serious athlete. Would you like to see a picture?"

"**YES!**" we all said, hurrying through Mr. Raymond's office to the main office.

Mrs. Spicer went into Mr. Naulty's office and came out a few moments later with an open book.

"It's his college yearbook," Mrs. Spicer explained. "You have to *promise* me you won't tell him I showed you."

"Sure," we agreed eagerly.

And we all crowded around the book and saw a black-and-white picture of a basketball player who looked *sort of* like Mr. Naulty, but about *half* his current—ahem—*thickness.*

"That's *him?*" Julian asked, looking closer.

"That's him," Mrs. Spicer confirmed.

"Wow, he looks really *different* now," Anika said in disbelief.

"He got HUGE!" Ursula said with wide eyes.

"Well, he hasn't been playing very much," Mrs. Spicer explained with a sigh. "He used to play after school with Mr. Camacho, the old basketball coach, years ago. But then that stopped, of course, when Mr. Camacho passed away..."

"But *now* Mr. Naulty has started playing again," Ursula said. "He plays in the gym after school. Didn't you know?"

Mrs. Spicer looked at Ursula with wide eyes.

"How did you find out?" Mrs. Spicer asked. "He's very private about it."

"*That's* for sure," Anika agreed. "Why?"

"Well, I guess he doesn't want people to see him play when he's so out of shape," Mrs. Spicer explained. "I'm surprised he let students see him."

"We didn't *see* him," I explained. "We just *heard* someone in there yesterday, and today we figured out it was him."

"It *was* him, wasn't it?" Anika asked.

"Yes, I'm sure it *was*," Mrs. Spicer nodded. "He *does* play on Wednesdays most weeks, and Fridays, too, when he can. But please don't tell him I told you."

"Oh, don't worry," I said with a smile, making a quick mental note of Mr. Naulty's basketball-playing schedule. "We won't say a word."

"And you won't either?" Mrs. Spicer asked Mr. Davidson and Mr. Raymond.

"My lips are sealed," Mr. Davidson said, making the mime move for zipping up his lips.

"Mine, too," Mr. Raymond agreed, zipping up *his* lips, too.

After that, we all left the office.

"Great work, guys," Mr. Davidson said to us when we were all in the hall.

"See, our investigation was *totally* worth it!" Ursula said. "*You* didn't think it would be!"

Ursula always liked to point out things like that.

"Yes, I'm definitely surprised. I never would've guessed Mr. Naulty was a basketball player," Mr. Davidson said, shaking his head in disbelief.

"I wish we could see him play," Blitz said. "*That* would be cool."

"Yeah," Julian agreed. "I wanna see if he's any good."

"Well, maybe next Wednesday I can arrange to stay after school with you in my office, and maybe we'll see him," Mr. Davidson said, checking his watch. "I have to run to rehearsal now, but we can talk about it next week."

After Mr. Davidson left to do his mime thing (or whatever it was he was rehearsing), we all stood there feeling good but not *great*.

"Next Wednesday is a *long* way away," Blitz said with a sigh.

"Well, guys," I said, "there's no reason we have to wait. Tomorrow's Friday, and Mrs. Spicer *did* say that Mr. Naulty played on Fridays. And we *do* have our plan with Blitz's alarm..."

"Let's do it!" Julian said with a sly smile.

"**YEAH!**" everyone else cheered.

"And *this* time, guys, let's stick to the plan, okay?" Blitz asked.

"Definitely," I agreed.

"You *said* it," Anika chimed in.

"Yeah, we don't want to get busted a *third* time," Ursula added.

And so it was settled: We had a plan, and we were sticking to it.

CHAPTER 10
THE PERFECT PLAN

The next day after school, we found Kelvin and told him the whole story.

"You're kidding me!" Kelvin said. "*He plays basketball? Mr. Naulty?*"

"The one and only!" I said.

"And he actually used to be good," Julian said.

"Or so Mrs. Spicer *says*," Ursula pointed out.

"But now he's all out of shape," Anika explained. "So he's embarrassed to let people see him play. That's why he sneaks around."

"But *we're* gonna try to see him today," Blitz said. "*If* he plays."

"Ooh," Kelvin said. "Sounds exciting!"

So we asked Kelvin to let us borrow a ladder, and fortunately he had one in the storage room. He helped us carry it out to the school yard so we could set up our alarm in the window.

Then we headed upstairs to the library to wait. The library was going to be open until 4:30 that afternoon because our librarian, Miss Butt (don't laugh), was ordering some new books. So we had plenty of time to hang out there—and we were willing to wait as long as necessary to catch a glimpse of our Principal Dribbler in action.

But as it turned out, it didn't take too long. Right around 3:20, we heard the giggling sound of Blitz's alarm.

Just in case the alarm had been set off by someone *other* than the Dribbler, Blitz and Julian ran downstairs first to take a quick peek inside the gym.

About five minutes later, we looked out the window and saw Blitz giving us the thumbs-up sign with a huge smile. So Ursula, Anika, and I grabbed all of our stuff, said goodbye to Miss Butt, and headed out.

When we got down to the school yard, Julian was up on the ladder, peeking into the gym, being really careful to keep his head hidden.

"He's just getting warmed up now," Blitz whispered. "He was doing all these toe-touches and leg stretches when *I* saw him! Oh, and he's wearing a big green headband! Wish I had my camera!"

Blitz was grinning ear to ear, totally thrilled to have seen Mr. Naulty looking so ridiculous.

"*Now* he's starting to take some shots," Julian whispered. "So far, he's sinking most of them, but they're pretty easy—*whoa*!"

Julian looked stunned. My first thought was that Mr. Naulty had fallen flat on his face.

"What?" we all whispered.

"He just did a turnaround jump shot," Julian said quietly. "*Nice.*"

And then Julian went back to watching in silence, his mouth hanging open in shock.

"You *guys*," he said, turning to us with wide eyes. "You're not gonna believe this, but he's actually GOOD!"

"*Really?*" we all asked.

"Let *us* see!" Ursula demanded in a harsh whisper. "You're hogging the ladder!"

So Julian finally climbed down, and the rest of us took turns climbing the ladder and watching. I have to say, I never expected to see what I saw...

SWOOSH

"Can you *believe it?*" Anika asked me when I came down off the ladder.

"No," I said, still trying to accept that the person who was shooting baskets like a pro was the same person who spent most of his time storming around the halls being unbearable.

"Pretty insane," Blitz said, nodding with wide eyes.

Once we'd all had a good look, Ursula brought Kelvin out so he could see Mr. Naulty in action. *He* was amazed, too.

By the time Mr. Naulty finished his workout and headed back into the locker room, we were all looking like this:

After we helped Kelvin put the ladder back in the storage room, we all piled up the stairs so we could go out the main exit. We were all talking excitedly, because for some reason, we felt like the coast was clear. We weren't even *thinking* about who might be leaving the building at the same time as we were...

MR. NAULTY, OF COURSE!

He was coming from the main office, just about to turn the corner to go out the main exit. He was carrying a basketball under one arm, and all those sweaty clothes from his locker under the other (guess he was finally going to wash them!). His hair was still wet from sweat, and his face was all red and shiny. To put it plainly, he looked *awful*. I could tell he was embarrassed to see us there.

We all got real quiet.

Fortunately, Mr. Naulty had no reason to yell at us, because the stairwell we were coming from was the same one that went up to the library. And we were *allowed* to be in the library after school, as Ursula would be the first to say. So Mr. Naulty just glanced quickly at us and then kept walking down the hall.

Then, suddenly, Julian spoke up.

"You play *basketball*, Mr. Naulty?" he asked.

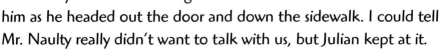

"Um, yes, I do," Mr. Naulty said, still walking quickly to the door.

We all ran to catch up with Mr. Naulty and walked alongside him as he headed out the door and down the sidewalk. I could tell Mr. Naulty really didn't want to talk with us, but Julian kept at it.

"Are you good?" Julian asked.

"Oh, no," Mr. Naulty said.

"I bet you are," Blitz said. "Did you, like, play in college?"

We all winced, thinking Blitz had said too much.

"Yes, I did, actually," Mr. Naulty said, looking surprised.

"So you *must've* been pretty good," Blitz said.

"Well, back *then* was a different story," Mr. Naulty said. "Basketball was my passion. I was preparing to make a career of it."

"*Then* what happened?" Julian asked.

"Oh, I had a knee injury," Mr. Naulty said. "And then I got out of shape and, well...things changed."

"And then you became a *principal?*" Anika asked.

"Isn't that kind of a...very different thing?" Ursula asked.

"Yeah, didn't you want to do something with *sports?*" Julian asked.

"Well, I *did* think about becoming a coach or a P.E. teacher," Mr. Naulty said. "But then I met someone who was a principal and decided *that* was the job I wanted."

"Do you *like* being a principal?" I asked.

"Sure," Mr. Naulty said with a shrug.

Not very convincing, if you ask me.

"But you know what?" Mr. Naulty said. "I'll tell you a little secret."

"What?" we asked.

"I've decided to become a basketball coach, too," Mr. Naulty said.

"You *have?*" Julian asked.

"Yes," Mr. Naulty said. "That's why I've been working on my game in the gym after school, so I'll be ready to coach in the fall."

"For which team?" Ursula asked.

"For our new school basketball team," Mr. Naulty said.

"WE'RE GONNA HAVE ONE?" Julian blasted. "Like, *definitely?*"

"Oh yes," Mr. Naulty said with a smile. "I think it's about time, don't you?"

"YES!" Julian said.

"We'll just have to do a little fundraising to get things started," Mr. Naulty said.

"*I* can handle that," Ursula said confidently. "Just tell me how much we need, and I'll come up with a business plan."

"Oh...all right, then," Mr. Naulty said, looking stunned. "Sounds like the team will be off to a good start."

"And *you're* going to be the coach?" Blitz asked, still looking shocked at the idea.

"Well, I don't think Mr. Davidson has much experience with basketball coaching," Mr. Naulty explained.

"*That's* for sure," Julian agreed.

"So I thought *I'd* do it, at least for the first year," Mr. Naulty said.

"*Wow,*" Julian said, looking like he was warming up to the idea.

"Well, we'll see how it goes," Mr. Naulty said, stopping in front of a little gray car and getting out his keys. "It was nice chatting with you."

Nice chatting with you? I could hardly believe my ears.

"This is your *car?*" Blitz asked, peeking in the windows. The car looked *way* too small for a big guy like Mr. Naulty.

"Indeed," Mr. Naulty said, throwing his stuff in the back and getting in the driver's seat. "Have a nice afternoon."

Have a nice afternoon? This was definitely a whole new side of Mr. Naulty we were dealing with. We all just stood there in shock, speechless, watching Mr. Naulty drive off in his little gray car.

CHAPTER 11
THE PHANTOMS ARE BORN

The next week at school, word got around about the basketball team. Everyone was totally psyched about it. I can't say the reaction was so great to the part about Mr. Naulty being the coach, though. *That* would take some getting used to. Mr. Naulty's approval ratings were generally in the zero range, as you can imagine.

But Julian wasn't going to let *that* ruin things. He was totally determined to get the team off to a good start, so he wanted to get pre-season training going right away. He managed to convince Mr. Naulty to let kids play basketball in the gym with him one day a week after school. I was pretty impressed that Julian managed to swing it.

Julian wasn't the *only* one who got things moving. Ursula came up with her "business plan" for fundraising, and Anika thought of a great name for the new team: "The Phantoms." Everyone really liked the new name, even Mr. Davidson, who thought it was perfect. Mr. Naulty, of course, had no idea why we would pick a name like that. And he never would!

So, that's about it for this operation. It was pretty amazing to find out that Mr. Naulty was actually good at something other than yelling (if you could call him "good" at that). And it was a *total* score to end up with a new basketball team. Even though *I'm* not that into basketball myself, I'm still really glad for Julian.

Anyway, I have to say, it helps a lot to know that Mr. Naulty is actually an okay guy...or at least not a total *bad* guy. Don't get me wrong—I'm not saying he's completely changed or anything. He still storms around school, yelling and being a royal pain in the neck. But now, when he does that, I just tune it all out and think of the Phantom Dribbler and his turnaround jump shot. Makes me smile, at least.

Until next time,

Spencer

Spy Gear Manual

Motion Detector

Siren sounds when an intruder is detected!

Sensor detects changes in light when someone walks past.

Detector Drill

To test your motion detector, place it on a table. Flip on the switch, and then wait three seconds for the detector to get ready. Then walk in front of the sensor. Were you detected? Try this from different distances and see how far away you can get and still be detected. Your detector should cover about 4 to 5 feet.

WOO! WOO!

Tip from Blitz:

Because your motion detector is sensitive to changes in light, it works best in brightly lit places.

Intruders Beware!

Want to know as soon as someone steps onto your turf? No problem. Set up your motion detector in your doorway, and you'll know right away when you have an intruder on your hands.

Pet Policer

Need to keep your dog off the couch? Set up your motion detector on the seat, and your dog will get an earful when he breaks the rules!

Keep Off My Desk!

Let your motion detector keep watch over your desk while you're in another room. If someone tries to touch your stuff, you'll find out!

How _else_ will your motion detector come in handy? It's up to you!

Have fun,
Spencer